KT-469-319

CLAUDE

at the Circus

ALEX T. SMITH

In a house on Waggy Avenue,
number 112, there lives a dog.

C015159946

For Nanna Betty
and her handbag full of
dog biscuits.

Text and illustrations copyright © 2012 Alex T. Smith
First published in Great Britain in 2012 by Hodder Children's Books

The right of Alex T. Smith to be identified as the Author and Illustrator of this Work has been asserted by him in accordance with the Copyright, Designs and Patents Act 1988.

FIRST EDITION

10 9 8 7 6 5 4 3 2 1

All rights reserved. Apart from any use permitted under UK copyright law, this publication may only be reproduced, stored or transmitted, in any form, or by any means with prior permission in writing from the publishers or in the case of reprographic production in accordance with the terms of licences issued by the Copyright Licensing Agency and may not be otherwise circulated in any form of binding or cover other than that in which it is published and without a similar condition being imposed on the subsequent purchaser.

All characters in this publication are fictitious and any resemblance to real persons, living or dead, is purely coincidental.

A catalogue record for this book is available from the British Library

978 0 340 99903 5

Printed and bound in China

The paper and board used in this paperback by Hodder Children's Books are natural recyclable products made from wood grown in sustainable forests. The manufacturing processes conform to the environmental regulations of the country of origin.

Hodder Children's Books
a division of Hachette Children's Books
338 Euston Road, London NW1 3BH
www.hachette.co.uk

A small dog.
A small, plump dog.
A small, plump dog who wears a beret and a rather fetching sweater.

His name is Claude, and here he is.

Claude's best friend is Sir Bobblysock. He is both a sock and quite bobbly.

Claude and Sir Bobblysock don't live in their big house all by themselves; Mr and Mrs Shinyshoes live there too.

Usually, Mr and Mrs Shinyshoes get up bright and early, leap into their smartest clothes and shiniest shoes and hotfoot it out of the door to work. Sometimes though, mainly on nice sunny Saturdays, Mr and Mrs Shinyshoes pop on their comfy clothes and pack a picnic.

'Let's go on a day trip!'
Mr Shinyshoes says.
'Lovely idea!' says Mrs Shinyshoes.
'Shall we take Claude?'

'No,' whispers Mr Shinyshoes.
'Let's leave him here to sleep.
You know how awfully tired he gets.
We won't be long.'

And so Mr and Mrs Shinyshoes
tiptoe out of the house,
hop in the car and pootle off
to the countryside for the day.

But Claude hasn't really been
asleep. He's been listening with
his floppy ears and peeping
with his beady eyes.

As soon as the front door closes,
Claude jumps out of bed, puts on
his beret, and decides what
adventure he shall have.

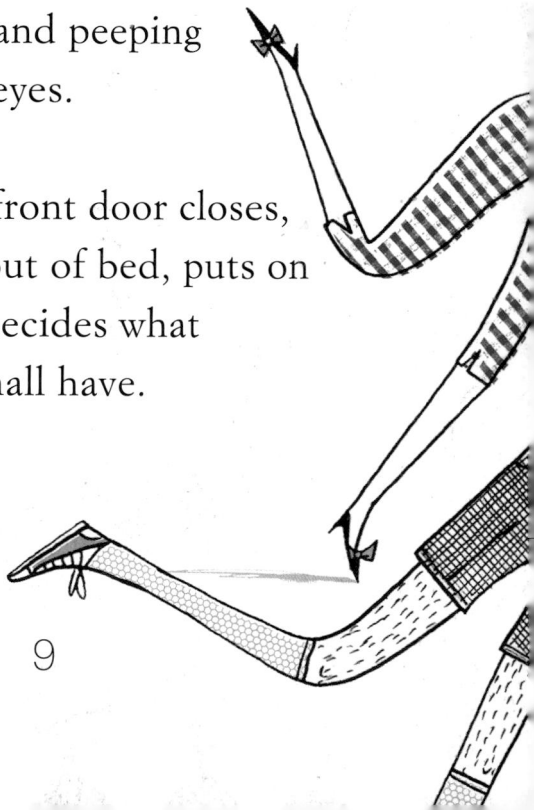

One bright Saturday morning when Mr and Mrs Shinyshoes were off in the country, Claude popped on his beret and thought about what he wanted to do. He felt like he needed a treat as he had been very busy the day before, giving his bed a good spring clean.

He had plumped up the pillow, shaken the blanket and tidied up his top-secret hidy-hole.

Out went several packets of half-chewed biscuits and a juicy bone baguette which was rather past its best.

Sir Bobblysock had sat in a comfy armchair and told him what to do. He would have loved to help, but he didn't want to get in the way.

'I think I will go to the park today,' Claude said.

So off he went.

Sir Bobblysock came along too, although he was worried that all the flowers might set off his hayfever and make him sneeze.

LOVELY PARK
AMAZING
ALAN'S
AMAZING
CIRCUS
HERE
TODAY!

Claude had never been to the park before.

He was surprised by how much like a big garden it was. There was grass absolutely everywhere and several trees, too.

And as it was such a sunny day, the whole place was full of people enjoying themselves.

SMALL SHALLOW HOLE
AMAZING ALAN'S AMAZING CIRCUS!
BIG TOP!
BANDSTAND
BIG DEEP HOLE
MR. SPRINKLE'S ICE CREAM VAN
GOLF COURSE
Claude is here!

SPOOKY WOOD
SMALL FIELD
PLAY AREA
BOATING LAKE
FLOWER BEDS
JAPANESE PAGODA
ROCKERY
CAFÉ
DUCK POND

Claude was pleased to see there was also a van selling ice creams. His tummy rumbled. Even though it wasn't quite eleven o'clock, he decided it was time for a snack.

But just as he and Sir Bobblysock stepped on to the path, a group of people in very strange clothes ran past them.

Claude had never seen anything like it.

There were even some people running with their babies in buggies!

Before he could say "excuse me" or ask politely what they were doing, he found himself tangled up amongst them.

Soon he and Sir Bobblysock were jogging along with the group. Sir Bobblysock had to hop like mad to keep up.

Round and round the park they went, running all the time. Claude quite enjoyed it, but he did wonder what on earth they were running for.

Had a lion escaped from the zoo?

Were all these people being chased by the police?

Maybe everyone had realised they weren't wearing proper clothes and were running home to get changed.

Claude didn't know.

What he did know was that his tummy was still grumbling and now he couldn't even see the ice cream van. There was nothing for it but to escape from all these mad running people.

Quickly, he tucked Sir Bobblysock under his arm, and was just about to leap out from the crowd when his foot got caught in one of the jogger's dangly shoelaces.

Everyone went flying. Claude and Sir Bobblysock hurtled through the air, bumped down on the grass and tumbled over and over until...

...they landed neatly in a flowerbed!

It was very comfortable there and the flowers smelt lovely.

Claude looked around and decided the flowerbed would be the perfect spot to take a nap. After all that running about, he and Sir Bobblysock were very tired.

Forgetting all about ice cream, Claude settled down and closed his eyes. Sir Bobblysock, who always found sleeping in sunlight difficult, popped on his eye mask and took some deep breaths to relax.

But the nap didn't last very long.

'Ahem! Ahem!' coughed a man in a smart uniform and a peaked cap. It was the park keeper, and he did not look happy.

Claude and Sir Bobblysock woke up.

Sir Bobblysock was not pleased.
He always liked to nap
for exactly forty-six
minutes, and he had
only managed five.

The park keeper didn't say anything. He just pointed to a sign that Claude hadn't seen earlier, when he had been flying through the air.

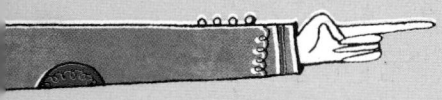

SLIGHTLY IMPOLITE NOTICE
DO NOT
SLEEP IN THE
FLOWERBEDS
THANK YOU

Claude sighed and stood up. He dusted down his lovely jumper, straightened his beret and set off along the path, with Sir Bobblysock hopping behind. Their nap would have to wait until later. It was time for ice cream!

Claude spotted the ice cream van in the distance.
'Come on!' he said to Sir Bobblysock, and marched towards it.

On the way they found themselves striding across a funny sort of field. There were holes everywhere in the grass and somebody had littered the place with balls.

Claude quickly filled up the holes and tidied the balls away under his beret.

Some very rude people didn't seem very happy about what he had done, so Claude and Sir Bobblysock quickly scampered away to the ice cream van.

18TH

When they got there, Claude bought himself a soft whippy ice cream with raspberry sauce and a chocolate flake. Sir Bobblysock really wanted a cup of tea but had a sticky, stripy lolly instead.

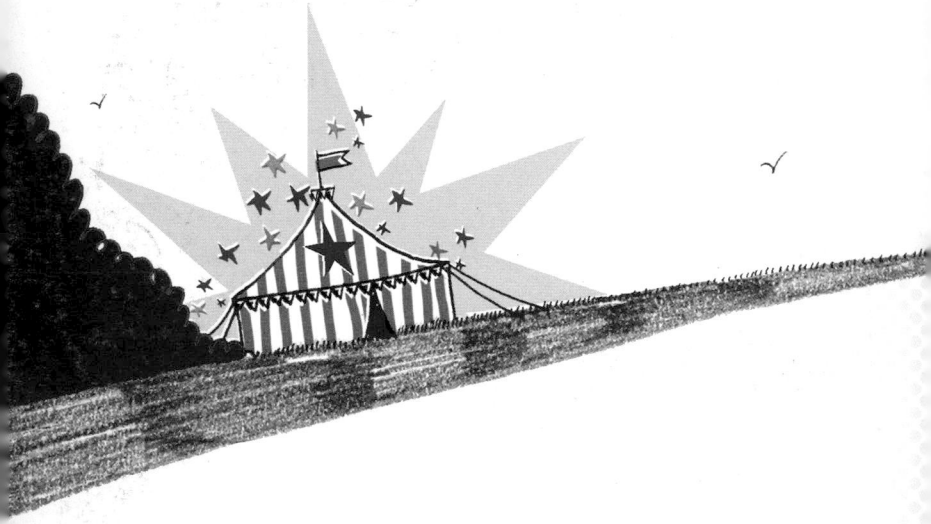

MR. SPRINKLES

After they had finished, Claude put Sir Bobblysock's lolly wrapper in the bin.

He also threw away another piece of rubbish he had found stuck to a bench, wanting to be helpful, and not wanting to get told off by the park keeper again.

They were wondering what to do next, when someone whizzed by on a scooter. And then someone else whizzed by.

It looked like fun, so Claude and Sir Bobblysock watched as the two children zipped here and there, doing tricky tricks and daredevil stunts.

'Would you like a go?' asked the little girl.

Claude nodded politely and climbed on to the scooter. He was a bit wobbly at first but was soon zooming about like nobody's business!

Sir Bobblysock had a turn, but he wasn't keen. He much preferred having a nice sit down and a biscuit.

Claude was just about to hand the scooter back to the little girl when he heard a noise from behind him. It was somebody shouting...

‘HE

LP!’

And a baby suddenly zoomed past!
One of the running mummies had
let go of her buggy!

The baby looked very happy,
but he was heading straight for the
duck pond.

'Quick!' shouted the little girl.
'Save him!'

Claude grabbed Sir Bobblysock and set off.

Sir Bobblysock took control of the handlebars, Claude pushed off with his foot along the path, and within a minute they had caught up with the escaped baby.

Claude reached out and caught the baby just before he fell in the water.

Everyone clapped and shouted, 'Hooray for Claude and Sir Bobblysock!'

Only the baby was a bit miffed because he had been enjoying his ride.

Claude pulled the balls he had tidied up earlier out from under his beret and gave them a quick juggle. Then Sir Bobblysock did a high-stepping jig.

Everyone laughed and cheered again, but Claude was beginning to feel rather shy so he and Sir Bobblysock went to find the café for a spot of lunch.

They were sitting outside, munching happily, when a very strange-looking man came and sat at the table next to them.

Claude did his very best not to stare, but of course Sir Bobblysock couldn't help himself. He turned right around in his seat and had a good look over the top of his hot dog. The man at the next table noticed.

'Hello,' he said, holding out his hand. 'I am the Amazing Alan, of Alan's Amazing Circus. May I offer you and your friend two tickets for this afternoon's performance? Ringside seats, on the house!'

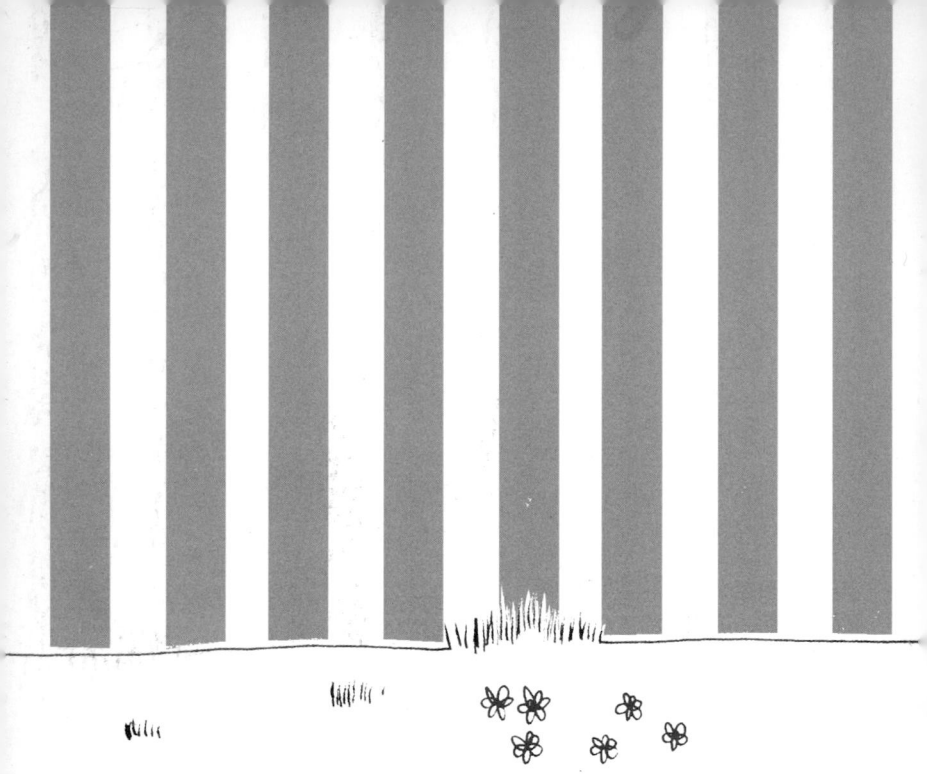

Claude was delighted, as he'd never been to the circus before. He and Sir Bobblysock decided to go to the circus tent early, to explore.

They ducked under the striped canvas.

All the performers were getting ready for the show in their caravans, so there was no one about.

Claude couldn't help noticing that although the tent was very exciting, it was also very untidy and quite grubby in places.

There was only one thing for it. He would have to give the tent a jolly good spring clean.

Claude fished a feather duster out from under his beret and dusted the ring. Then he swept all the sawdust on the floor into a big pile in the centre. He climbed a long ladder and gave the trapeze a good polish, and the high wire a once over with a damp cloth.

Behind a curtain, he found a pile of plates covered in fluffy custardy cream. Claude decided the cream smelt a bit funny, so he threw it away and washed up the plates. Soon they were all neatly stacked in a pile, sparkling clean.

By now the rest of the audience had started to come in, so Claude and Sir Bobblysock took their seats. The Amazing Alan waved to them, but he had to hurry off to help the Human Cannonball find her glittery crash helmet.

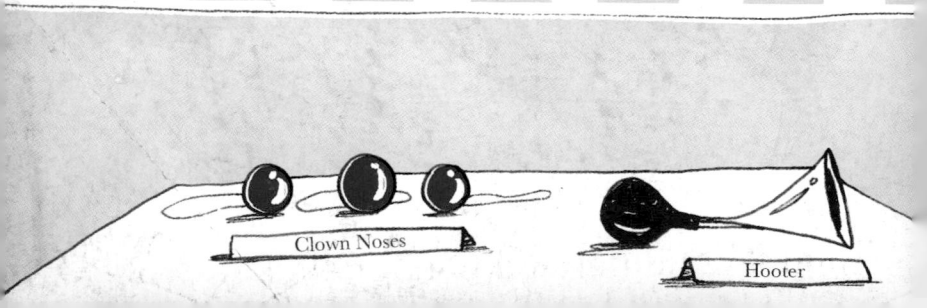

BACKSTAGE
Custard Pies

Claude and Sir Bobblysock watched in amazement as acrobats and gymnasts and dancers and clowns came tumbling into the ring. They were all dressed in wonderful costumes. Sir Bobblysock, who liked sequins and feathers and that sort of thing, was very impressed. The Amazing Alan cracked his whip, and the show began.

But it was a disaster!

The clowns weren't funny at all. Their custard pies had been washed up, and when they threw the clean plates at each other they ended up with sore noses.

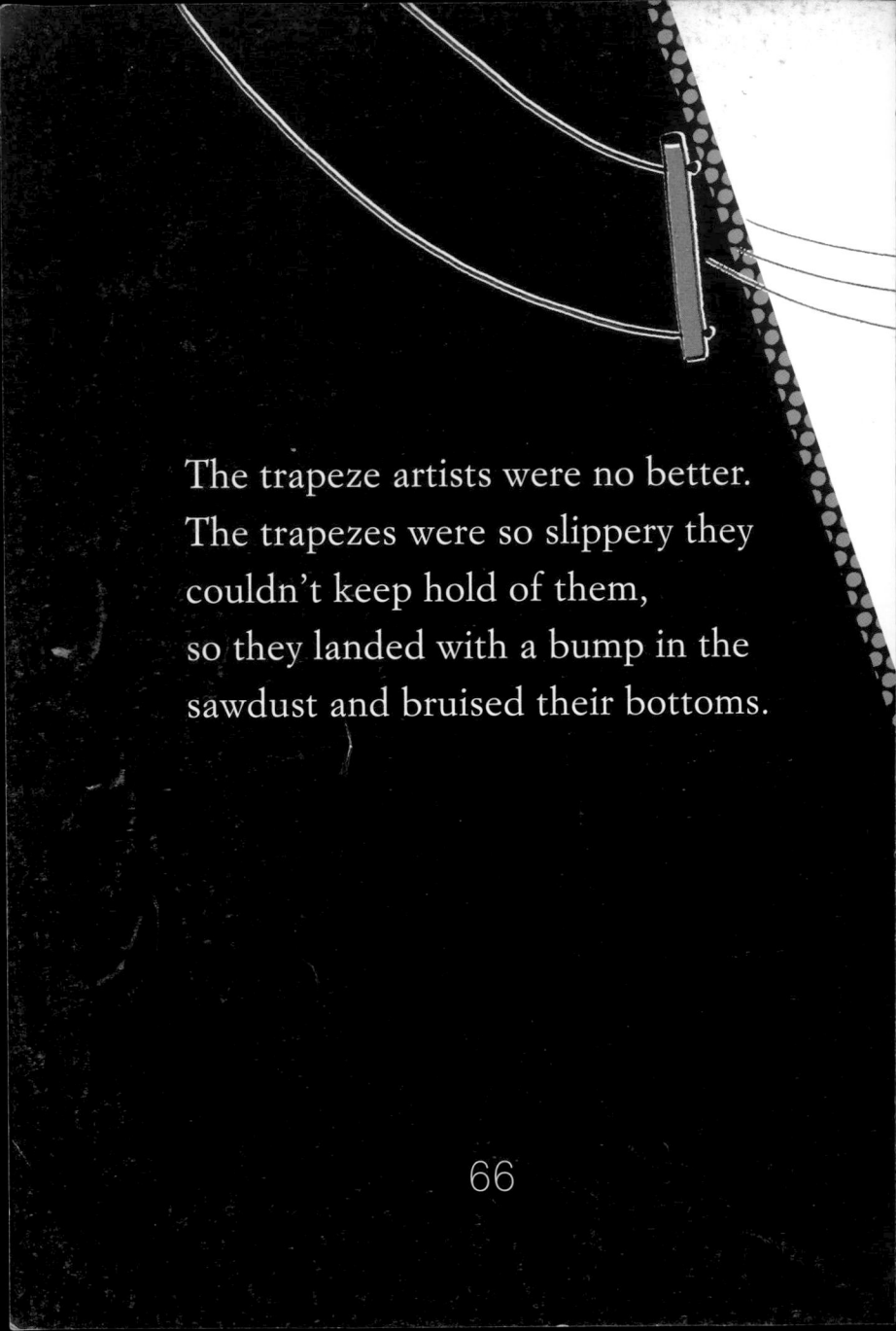

The trapeze artists were no better.
The trapezes were so slippery they
couldn't keep hold of them,
so they landed with a bump in the
sawdust and bruised their bottoms.

The audience began to realise something was wrong.

The tightrope walker slipped off the damp wire and dangled by her knickers until their elastic snapped. Then she fell on to a trampoline, bounced through the tent roof and landed in the duck pond.

People in the audience began to mutter, and the Amazing Alan was very embarrassed.

'This has never happened before,' he apologized to Claude and Sir Bobblysock. 'I've got no idea what's wrong with my performers today.'

Claude did, and was beginning to feel a bit hot behind the ears.

'Would you take over?' Alan asked. 'Otherwise, I'm afraid the audience will ask for their money back.'

Claude was astonished. He had never performed in a circus before.

'Don't worry, you'll be brilliant,' said Alan. 'I saw you juggling in the park. Here, wear this hat. And take the little fellow with you – he's funny.'

So Claude and Sir Bobblysock found themselves standing in the middle of the ring...

At first Claude wasn't sure what to do, so he just smiled politely and wagged his tail.

'Get on with it!' hissed the Amazing Alan, who was watching nervously.

Claude smiled again, then he did some star jumps and some twirling around on the spot.

The audience was impressed.

Then Claude cleverly rubbed some chalk on the bottom of his shoes, so his feet wouldn't slip.

He clambered up the ladder and stepped on to the tightrope.
It was ever so high, so he shut his eyes and pretended he was just tip-toeing down a very thin bit of road.

To his surprise, he found that he was quite good at it. He hung from one paw and stood on one leg (not at the same time).

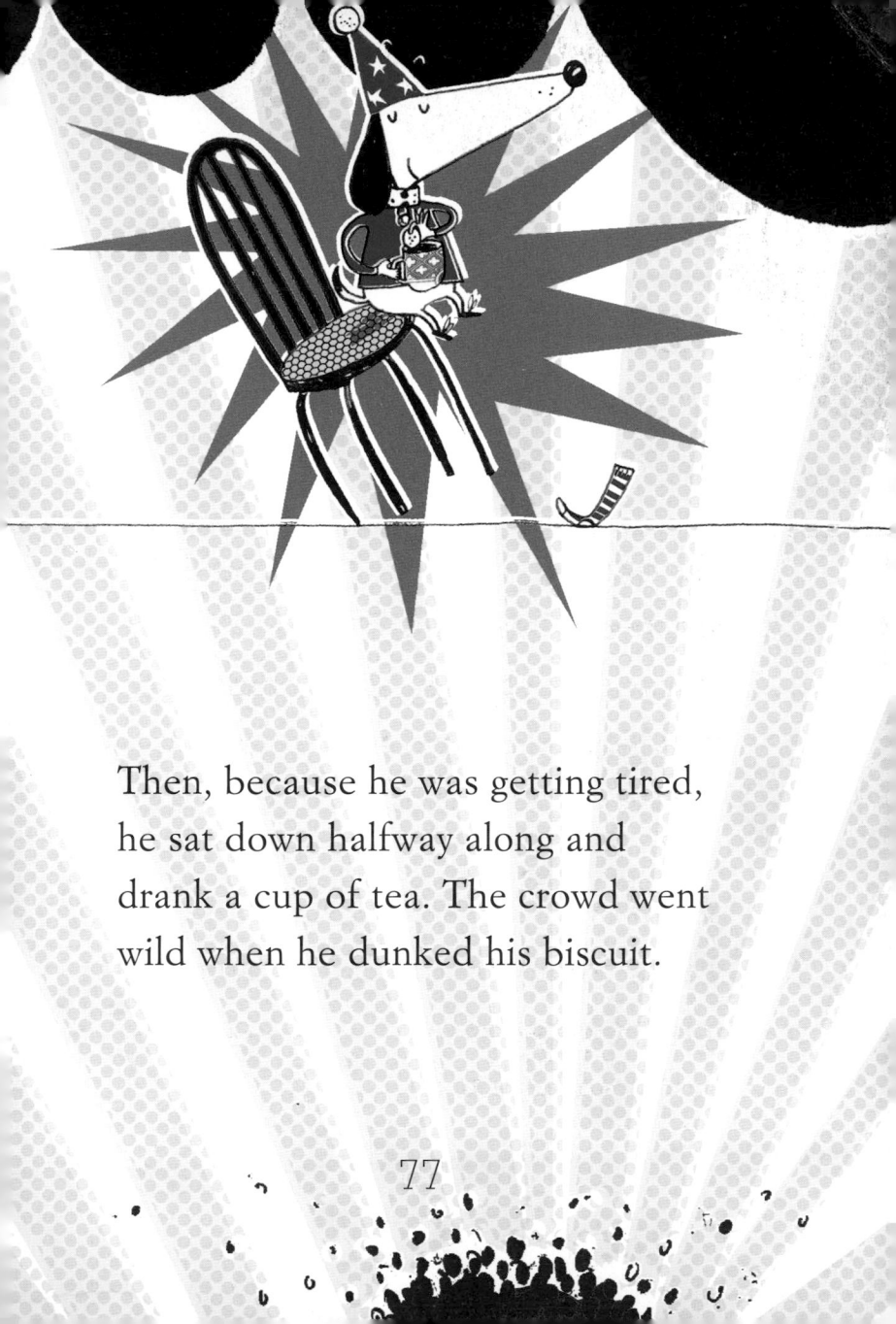

Then, because he was getting tired, he sat down halfway along and drank a cup of tea. The crowd went wild when he dunked his biscuit.

Next, Claude and Sir Bobblysock did a clown routine. They whizzed around the ring in a car that was too small for them, and fell over a lot.

Then they threw some freshly-made custard pies at each other. The pies were so delicious, Claude couldn't help catching one in his mouth and gobbling it up (plate and all!).

The audience thought this was very funny.

Finally, it was time for the trapeze act.

Bravely, Claude and Sir Bobblysock climbed up the ladders, reached for a trapeze each, took a deep breath and swung out over the audience.

They were marvellous, flying through the air like a couple of monkeys!

Everyone leapt to their feet and clapped until their hands were sore. 'Hooray!' they cried. 'Hooray for Claude and Sir Bobblysock!'

The Amazing Alan was delighted. 'You are both absolute stars!' he boomed, as Claude and Sir Bobblysock took a bow.

'Please will you join our circus? You will be very famous if you do!'

Claude thought for a moment. Although circus life sounded fun, he would miss Mr and Mrs Shinyshoes too much if he went away. So he said thank you very much and that he had enjoyed himself a lot, but he would rather just go home. Besides, Sir Bobblysock was in need of one of his long lie-downs.

Suddenly Claude gasped. There was a problem! He had forgotten the time.

How could he get home before Mr and Mrs Shinyshoes came back from the country?

Luckily the Human Cannonball had an idea.

As soon as Claude had said his goodbyes to all the friendly circus people, he put on the Human Cannonball's glittery crash helmet, tucked Sir Bobblysock safely up his jumper, and clambered into the huge cannon.

BOO

MIT!

Claude flew through the air and
landed with a CRASH
in his cosy bed in the kitchen,
just as Mr and Mrs Shinyshoes were
opening the front door.

He quickly pretended to be asleep.

'Um... Mrs Shinyshoes?' said Mr Shinyshoes, looking at Claude. 'Do you happen to know why Claude is wearing a glittery crash helmet?'

'No idea, darling!' said Mrs Shinyshoes, looking up. 'Do you know why there's a Claude-shaped hole in the roof?'

Mr Shinyshoes said he didn't have a clue.

But Claude did, so he gave Sir Bobblysock a secret wink.

How to be a Clown

1. Paint your nose red with face paints.
2. Tell some silly jokes.

What kind of dog takes a bubblebath?

A shampoodle!

What swings from a trapeze and miaows?

An acrocat!

Why do dogs wag their tails?

Because no one else will do it for them!

3. Fall over a lot.

TA-DA! You are now a clown!

Remember to keep your eye out for Claude and Sir Bobblysock. You never know where they might pop up next!